BITS OF THE DEAD

edited by
Keith GOUVEIA

illustrated by
SEAN SIMMONS

COSCOM ENTERTAINMENT
WINNIPEG

COSCOM ENTERTAINMENT
130 Stanier Street
Winnipeg, MB R2L 1N3 Canada

ISBN – 10 1-897217-81-1
ISBN – 13 978-1-897217-81-8

PUBLISHED BY COSCOM ENTERTAINMENT
www.coscomentertainment.com
Text set in Garamond; Printed and bound in the USA
COVER ART AND INTERIOR ILLUSTRATIONS BY SEAN SIMMANS

Library and Archives Canada Cataloguing in Publication

Bits of the dead / edited by Keith Gouveia ; illustrated by Sean Simmans.

ISBN 978-1-897217-81-8

1. Horror tales, American. 2. Horror tales, Canadian. 3. Horror tales, English. 4. American fiction—21st century. 5. Canadian fiction (English)—21st century. 6. English fiction—21st century. 7. Zombies—Fiction. I. Gouveia, Keith, 1975- II. Simmans, Sean, 1970-

PN6071.H727B58 2008 813'.087380806 C2008-903542-9

INNARDS

BITS OF THE DEAD

MMVIII

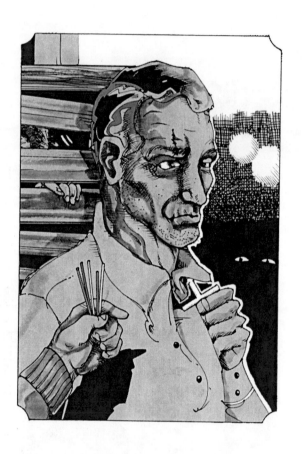

Lee Thomas

TUESDAY

The irony was lost on none of them as they drew straws. Six of them sat before the fire, hands trembling as they plucked the matches from one boy's fist. Outside, their attackers groaned and pounded on the walls of the cabin.

They'd thought the mountains would give them isolation from the plague, and to some degree it had. There weren't many of the ravenous dead at their door, but there were enough, especially since those inside were fragile.

The food had run out last Tuesday—a week ago, now. Empty cabinets and cupboards. Even the occasional insect eluded their desperate fingers and their saliva-soaked tongues. The six understood the hunger fueling the dead outside. The short straw would fix that, if the remaining five were brave enough to eat.

Nate Southard
ANOTHER LONESOME DAY

They don't want me.

As recently as a week ago, I considered that a ridiculous thought. They don't want me? That's not even possible. I'd watched them tear apart and devour every living thing unlucky enough to get too close. I saw it on the television—back before the stations went dead—and from the safety of my window.

For awhile, I convinced myself it was luck, a dumb turn of the universe that kept me alive while the rest of the world walked around on dead legs.

I know better now. They don't want me.

I walk through them every single day. I smell their rot-stink and get close enough to see the flies crawl across their mottled skin. I've made this journey naked. I've rubbed raw hamburger on my skin. They keep ignoring me. I am not a morsel they want to eat. I am tainted, inedible.

I'm not worth the effort.

My parents didn't think so. Neither did my teachers. They all called me a lost cause. And Roger . . . I still can't stand to think about Roger. It hurts too much.

I held one of the dead today. I wrapped my arms around its decaying body and waited for it to bite. It never did. I thrust my forearm into the gaping maw of another, but it never bit down on me. It didn't even react when I lowered my face to its decomposing shoulder and cried.

They don't want me.

I'm not worth the effort.

Guess I'll just sit in my apartment, same as I always have. I thought the plague would change things, but it didn't. It's not fair.

The world's over, and it's just another lonesome day.

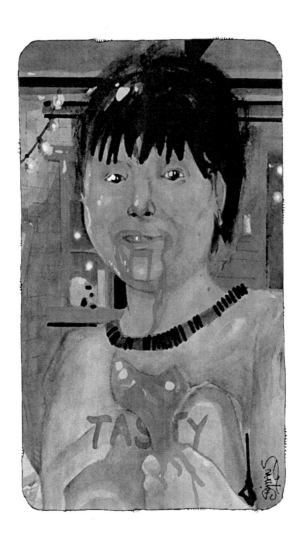

Piers Anthony

THE COURTING

"I come to court you," she said.

Jason looked up from his desk, startled. He knew June only passingly, a secretary in an adjacent office. She had a starlet quality face and body, so naturally had no interest in an ordinary Joe like him. Was this some cruel tease?

"I really am not in the mood at the moment," he said.

"I need to make love with you now." She spoke in somewhat measured tones.

She couldn't be serious. "Not now. I have a headache."

"I know. This must be fast." She opened her blouse.

"There is a catch."

Of course there was. At any other time he would have been seriously interested, despite his suspicion that she was playing a game. At this point he just wanted to get rid of her, because his headache was getting worse. "Catch?"

"I am a zombie."

This jolted his headache into the background for an instant. Her exposed skin didn't indicate she was dead. It was peach-colored, just like his. Maybe a little pale, but that was it. "You can't be."

"The peripherals are the first to go. My hair is a wig." She lifted it, showing her bald pate briefly. "My teeth, false." She lifted out her denture, as briefly. "My eyes have contact lenses. My nails are glued on. But my core body remains solid flesh. That is what counts, for this."

"But—but zombies—if one even touches a living person, he dies horribly."

"True, in essence." She put her cold hand on his.

Jason was so startled and dismayed that his bladder let go. He ignominiously wet himself, there at his desk.

"Gotta go!" he said, lurching up and lumbering to the men's room. His headache was worse than ever.

In the men's room he hauled off his sodden trousers and undershorts and put them in the sink to rinse. Everything was going wrong!

"You are starting a stroke," June said behind him. She had followed him in! "You will die in minutes. Clasp me now, and not only will your expiring life force restore me for another month, you will become a zombie and be able to continue your existence. Few others will notice. It is better than dying."

He turned to stare at her, suddenly believing. She had stripped, and she was correct: her central body was in excellent shape. "That's why you came to me! You knew!"

"Yes. I need your essence." She stepped into him, drawing him close as his head seemed to swell with pain.

Then the pain faded, and there was only June and the phenomenal urgency of their love. Becoming a zombie no longer seemed so bad. For one thing, it was pain free.

Michael Laimo
IT'S A SHAME IT HAD TO END LIKE THIS

She screams.

They scream.

She's here in the house with me.

The zombies are outside, tearing at the barricades, the aluminum siding.

They know, somehow, that I'm in here. Do they smell me? The blood from my injuries? *How do they know?*

She's in the bedroom. I've locked the door but she's pounding at it, screaming, moaning, screaming, moaning.

My wife.

Outside the zombies wait, knowing that, at some point, I need to leave here. To find food.

I haul the axe over my shoulder, and move to the bedroom.

Where my wife is.

Screaming, moaning.

I can hear her, clawing at the locked door. Trying to get out.

I've put off this moment far too long.

With no further hesitation, I raise my booted foot and kick in the door. Splinters fly. So does my wife. She falls back in odd silence, grunting as she crashes down to the bloody carpet.

Her eyes roll up toward mine, insane.

I bring the axe down, aiming for the head, hoping for a clean cut, hoping to quickly end it all. She moves sideways. Screaming. The axe comes down on her shoulder instead, severing her arm from her body. Blood geysers from both exposed wounds.

Her screams are deafening. I attempt to end them with another swing of the axe. This time my aim is bad, and I lop off her other arm.

It twitches as though alive itself. More blood spouts.

Outside, the ghouls continue to wail, to scratch at the barricades over the windows, the house's aluminum siding.

My wife continues to claw at the carpet, eyes rolling in their sockets, attempting to focus. If I'm to get past those things outside, then I'm gonna have to get it right the first time.

One blow to the head is all it takes.

I swing the axe back up over my shoulder, and in a fluid arc, bring it back down, slicing into my wife's neck.

Her head flies across the room, knocking into the wall before plummeting down with a dull thud on the carpet. Blood fountains up from the stump left behind before trickling down into a slow dribble, her life now extinguished.

The zombies scratch at the barricade, akin to all the activity inside the house.

There must be a dozen or more of them out there.

How am I gonna get past them?

Gotta get it right the first time. One swing, to take the head off.

I've had very little practice.

My wife . . .

Thing is . . . she was *alive.*

I wasn't going to let them get to her. I wasn't going to let her come back as one of those things.

"Rest in peace," baby I say aloud, thinking, *It's a shame it had to end like this.*

I rest the bloody axe on my shoulder, then head outside to get it right the first time.

Joel Arnold

ROTTEN FRUIT

A figure sat beneath the large, leafy apple tree in the distance. A woman, judging by the sundress and floppy hat, but Jackson stayed back, studying her, just to make sure. The woman fanned herself with an old red Frisbee, and the movement of her hand and wrist seemed too smooth, too human to be one of *them*.

Jackson swallowed. He hadn't seen a woman, a real woman, for so long. His jaw dropped at the sight of her calves, feminine and lovely. Definitely human. But to be safe, he stayed in place behind the thick, fragrant lilac bush he was using for cover, only straightening up enough so that she could see his face.

"Hey!" He waved.

She slowly turned her head.

Definitely human—he could see that from here.

She looked terrified of him.

"It's okay," he called. "I'm not one of them." Wasn't it obvious? He held up his hands to show her he wasn't armed, and stepped out from behind the lilacs. He glanced around the open field, making sure there was no one else—no *thing* else—coming.

As he neared, he noticed dozens of fallen apples, shriveled and rotting, surrounding her. She slowly shook her head as he approached.

Jackson smiled. "Don't be afraid. I won't hurt you." He studied her carefully. Her cheeks were flush, eyes clear, the hand waving the Frisbee intact, the skin supple, fingernails clean and trimmed. "What's your name?"

She didn't answer.

19

He stepped closer, breathing in the sickly sweet apple smell. "My name's Kenneth Jackson. I promise I won't hurt you."

She waved the Frisbee faster and closed her eyes.

She's terrified, Jackson thought. *Maybe I should just let her be.* But didn't she know how much danger she was in? Just sitting there all alone?

He stepped closer. The woman opened her eyes, turning her face to the green leaves and ripe, red fruit clinging to the branches above. A tear glistened on her cheek. Jackson held his hands out to show her again that he meant no harm. He approached tentatively. She continued to slowly shake her head, as if trying to escape a bad dream.

He stepped beneath the leafy canopy of the apple tree and noticed a chain circling her waist, holding her fast to the rough trunk. He stopped, confused. She opened her mouth and grunted. Her tongue was missing. She shook her head faster, and glanced into the canopy once again.

Jackson's eyes followed hers.

They were there, waiting.

Before he could move, three pairs of rotting hands shot out from above, grabbing him by the head and shoulders. Branches shook. Apples fell. Three desiccated, disfigured creatures dropped from their perches, their teeth tearing into the rind of Jackson's skull, searching for the fresh fruit of his brain.

The woman closed her eyes and grimaced at the sounds of crunching bone, waving her Frisbee faster and faster.

James Newman

REUNION

The dead pound at the lids of their coffins, scratch at the walls of their tombs.

It's how I imagined Hell might sound, when I was a churchgoing man.

The cemetery covers three sprawling acres adjacent to my backyard. Their screams are muffled . . . yet there are *so many* of them, I'm often forced to wear earplugs if I want to sleep at night.

I wipe sweat from my wrinkled brow and keep digging.

* * *

Those old drive-in flicks I used to drag Dorothea to when we were spring chickens, they got it wrong.

It's not like they all burst from their graves the moment "it" happened. Except for the cadavers that were lying in funeral homes or morgues, *most* of the dead are contained. How easy can it be for something that's been decomposing for decades to escape from its coffin, much less swim through six feet of earth? Physically impossible, far as I can figure.

At least without help.

But here's where the picture-shows really screwed up: The cities aren't overrun with packs of ravenous zombies constantly overtaking the living, playing tug-of-war with intestines, fighting over chunks of fresh brain.

In fact, you *can* walk among them.

Because they only come after you if they're *hungry*.

They're not always hungry. Not *all* of them, every second of the day.

They mostly just stumble around. Mostly.

They only come after you if they haven't eaten in a while. That's when you gotta be careful.

* * *

Eleven months ago, my wife of sixty years passed away. Cancer.

I thought my world had ended the day Dorothea left me.

Little did I know that, when the End of the World finally did come, I would be with her again.

* * *

Their screams become more audible the deeper I dig. They drown out everything: the wind whispering through the trees on the far side of the cemetery, my own labored breathing.

They know I'm here, and they want me to let *them* out, too.

Still . . . Nothing from *her.* My darling is silent. But I know she is waiting for me.

The blade of my shovel strikes metal. My ancient heart skips a beat.

"Dorothea," I cry, "I'm here!"

A gentle tapping from inside her casket, as if in response. It makes me smile, and this old man hasn't smiled for many months.

At last, I toss my shovel aside. I bend, scraping the remaining clumps of dirt from her coffin with my trembling, arthritic hands.

"Not much longer now, my love . . ."

I ponder what life will be like, having her near me again.

Meanwhile, I try not to think about . . . *other* things.

Like . . . what will happen when she starts to make the same sounds as the *rest* of them.

When my darling Dorothea grows hungry, I know I will do what I have to do.

I will have no choice but to feed her.

Somehow.

Christopher Allan Death

SPECIAL DELIVERY

A clump of innards hung from the box; greasy, bloody, steaming innards that quivered with every step. It wasn't the most eloquent packing job John had ever seen, but it was sure tantalizing. All those tender kidneys and juicy hearts made his mouth water.

He tucked the box under his arm as he approached the front steps.

"Delivery," he called through a mouthful of broken teeth. He would have tried the doorbell but his left arm was severed at the elbow, revealing a mass of twisted tendon and broken bone; the result of his service in the zombie war.

"Anyone home?"

The door cracked open and a little girl stood inside. She was pretty—all sunken blue eyes and gnarled skin. The kind he saw in television commercials and magazines. But she wasn't perfect. Her dress was tattered and her left foot was missing; probably from an anti-personnel mine.

"Rebecca Hall?" he asked.

"Yes," she said.

Even in the shadows, she looks like him.

"I have a package from your father."

"Daddy?" she exclaimed. "My daddy sent me a *present?*"

John nodded awkwardly and extended the box toward her. His joints were becoming more and more inflexible, so it took a moment to complete the task.

He hated rigor mortis.

"What is it?" she asked, eyeing the gooey contents hungrily.

"It's a gift," John said. "Your father asked me to give it to you in case something should happen."

Rebecca reached into the writhing knot of innards and fingered a particularly greasy length of intestine. "What do you mean?" she asked. "The war is over, isn't it?"

"Yes," John replied. "The war is over. And we won."

"Then where is my daddy?" she pressed.

John looked at the box of steaming innards sadly (or hungrily; at the moment he couldn't tell) and sighed. "You're holding him," he said.

The effects of his words were almost instantaneous. Rebecca crumbled to her knees and began to cry; a dry, throaty sob that shook her diminutive frame. But her sadness wouldn't last long, and John knew it.

Soon she would forget the incident and become her happy undead self again. She would skip down the street and play with her undead dolls.

Like a typical twelve-year-old girl.

She was a resilient kid, and while her father's death would be hard to digest at first, it would go down much easier than his remains.

John Weagly
DUET OF THE LIVING DEAD

Two zombies. One brain.

Chunks of flesh littered the farmhouse floor; arms and legs, feet and fingers, but only one remaining brain.

Jack and Dianne both gazed at it. They growled, limped toward each other and met over the shattered skull that served as the delicacy's serving platter.

Two zombies. One hunger.

From out of the meat on his right thigh, like a king and a sword and a stone, Jack pulled a serrated carving knife, a souvenir from the fight. With the grace of a dead surgeon, with the lifeless affection of lovers departed, he cleaved the brain in two. Jack gave Dianne the bigger half.

She grunted her appreciation.

Two zombies. One heart.

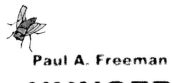

Paul A. Freeman

HUNGER

Tied to a chair, I'm racked with thirst and hunger! Yet bound as I am I can't appease these appetites. And even if I were free, my daughter Heidi is pointing the barrel of a .38 Special at my head.

The gun quivers in her trembling hand. "I can't do it, Mum," she says. "It doesn't matter what he's become. He's still Dad."

"No, he isn't!" Jill corrects. "Now he's just like one of those monsters outside. The father you know is gone. This creature's an empty shell of the man we once loved. He only wants one thing from us. In your heart of hearts, you know it's true."

I strain at my bindings, make an inarticulate moaning sound and almost topple the chair.

"See!" says my wife. "He's a mindless beast, driven by the same instinct as the rest of them—the instinct to kill. He wouldn't think twice about tearing us limb from limb."

Somewhere in the recesses of my brain I recall a church and a wedding, a hospital and a birth. The love I hold for the family I'm about to lose forever overwhelms me, and in spite of my insatiable thirst, moisture drips from my eyes.

"Look!" Heidi bawls. "Dad's crying. He recognizes us."

Jill takes charge of the .38 and tells Heidi to leave the room. She has one last act of kindness to perform and doesn't want our daughter to witness it.

The door closes behind the blubbering teenager and I'm alone with my wife.

Jill lowers the gun and puts it on the table. She moves behind me, crouches down and undoes my bindings. "Go!" she instructs me. "Go and join the others like you. Sooner or later the scientists will discover a cure. They're sure to. Then I'll come and find you. We'll change you back to normal. I promise."

I stagger to my feet, turn, hold out my arms to my beautiful wife. There are tears in her eyes, too.

This is Jill, I tell myself. *My darling Jill.*

She hugs me, and my breast is bursting with a husband's love. But the affection suddenly fades, overpowered by those baser instincts I've so newly acquired. In place of love I'm once again thirsty—and unbearably hungry. My lips touch Jill's neck and below them I feel the rhythmical pulse of blood flowing through a main artery.

My mouth opens.

Minutes later, when Jill reanimates, we look into each other's eyes. There's a brief moment of clarity and understanding. We've always loved our daughter and will do whatever's best for her—no matter what that might involve.

Heidi is tapping at the door with a combination of concern and impatience. "Mum? What's going on in there?" she says, finally opening the door. "What's taking so long?"

We rush towards our beloved daughter, happy in the knowledge that we'll soon be a family unit again.

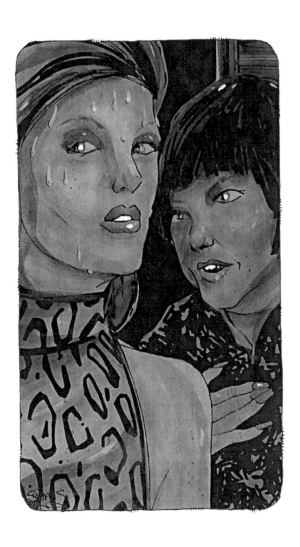

Drew Brown

RUN

Peter drummed his fingers against the dashboard. He wished the radio still played music instead of the endless cycle of the emergency broadcast.

He wished his wife hadn't chosen the fast lane; they'd hardly moved in hours, hemmed in by cars and the central reservation. He wondered how far back the jam stretched behind them, and how long it would be before they could move freely to the coast.

"Mummy, I need a wee."

"You'll have to wait, Luke."

In the wing-mirror, Peter watched a man come running between the lines of stationary traffic. Heavy footsteps pounded the tarmac as the man continued up the road.

"Mummy? Daddy?"

Peter adjusted the rear-view mirror. The image was filled with a swarm of people, all on foot, overtaking the cars. They were panicking and scared, streaming up the carriageway.

A woman paused to bang on the windscreen. "They're here," she shouted, before vanishing into the passing crowd.

Peter bit his fingernails, trying to hide the trembling of his hands. He looked around at the nearby cars and found the occupants were leaving, abandoning their vehicles and possessions.

"Pete?" His wife made the single word sound like a question. She turned the key to silence the engine.

He knew what she was asking and nodded his head.

"Yes."

She opened her door and slipped outside.

The cold, smoggy air entered the car. The back door opened and Luke was pulled from the rear seat. The boy began to cry.

Peter watched his wife leave, carrying their son.

He didn't blame her. And she had at least closed the doors. He leaned across and engaged the locks.

In the rear-view mirror, he caught sight of his wheelchair, securely stowed in the luggage compartment.

He looked down at his enfeebled legs and waited.

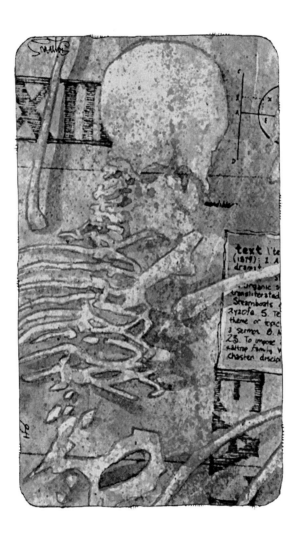

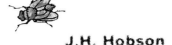

J.H. Hobson

BAD GIRL

I shouldn't have gone out after the alerts. I know. I should have waited for the All-Clear. But, after a while, you get . . . I don't know . . . used to them. You start thinking, "What? Undead in my neighborhood again? Who cares? I need to get some Nyquil and I'm going out to get it right now."

I didn't see her until it was almost too late. She was on the other side of my BMW-740, standing still, just looking at it. Maybe she used to go for rides in one of these. Since the "Crisis" hit the suburbs, cars like this have been cheap to pick up, being as rich zombies can't drive anymore than the poor ones.

She was probably good looking. Once. Not now. Now she looked a little rough around the collar. Particularly where her fur was rotting off and her ears were gone.

Anyway, there she was. And there I was. I backed up slow, really slow, right back up into the house. Then I locked the door and called Animal Cadaver Control. Took them about ten minutes to answer, but they finally sent a man over.

I looked out my window. She'd ambled over toward the curb, just sort of walking around, going nowhere in particular. She looked sort of lost. You'd almost feel sorry for her. Almost.

Until you saw the way she up and tore open the guy from ACC. Which serves them right for employing the

41

inept, but now there's two of them out there. It'll be hours before another agency will dispatch anyone.

I still don't have my cough medicine.

Julia Sevin

THE SHUNNED

Abel will not take another step.

We've come to the blueberries beyond the barley fields. The crushed fruit makes a foul mash underfoot.

"Son," pleads Gregor, "show us."

Abel is nine, but insolent as a small child now with tears in his eyes. He shakes his head and my hand itches to strike him.

Gregor waves and the child runs home.

"You spoil him," I say.

"He has already told us where." He wipes the sweat from his reddening face. "Jacob is fine, do you think . . ."

"Jacob *is* fine," I spit. "I *raised* him fine."

We continue walking. I have my largest shovel and Gregor carries a hammer. The bushes shiver and thousands of ripe berries fall to the earth. A waste.

It's been years now since *die Plage*, maybe four. For two months we were all well. Then the reporter and his men came in with their questions and coughing. Before long, Ruth's father had *ein Dämon*, then Abraham Schrager and Elizabeth Nussbaum. We tried to drive out *die Dämonen* but their bodies were all too weak and their spirits relented to corruption. We built a place for them, *der Vermiedenhaus*. No more than plain pine buildings surrounded by a high fence.

We raised fences all around our land. Sometimes, English hunters used ladders.

Now Gregor's face is as red as meat and wet with tears.

"Discipline yourself," I say.

Abel and my son, Jacob, all of five years, came to harvest the blueberries before they rotted. They saw something that frightened Abel like a cat. He abandoned my son under the black walnut where the berry bushes grow tall, fifty paces from *der Vermiedenhaus*. It's close now, and we must step lightly.

The stench of fermenting berries makes me lightheaded. If Gregor doesn't give Abel a thrashing tonight, I surely will.

* * *

I smell its filth first.

Tucked beneath a bramble, it's easy to miss. The cold has kept it fairly whole. Its vest was once unnatural orange, but a long autumn has collected on it. Nearby is the head, separate and snapping. A large basket is overturned with berries spilling from under the lid.

Gregor looks about. "So careless, to shoot a thing high in the spine and simply leave it."

Red blood musses its lipless mouth. I consider crushing its head in one blow and putting an end to the wild-eyed gnashing. I think I would hear the *Dämon* skitter away among the brambles.

I roll the head into the basket. A ribbon of pale green—Ruth's favorite color, the color of her wedding dress, her someday burial dress—is woven round the handle. I use it to tie the lid closed. Gregor drags the body by the arms, whispering prayers. The thing's teeth grind louder.

We reach *der Vermiedenhaus*. I pitch the basket over the fence. They groan and curse. I hear Frau Nussbaum's wet shriek.

Ruth will be sorry to see her basket lost.

Gregor shouts.

I turn, and my son stands here. His hat is gone and his ankle is bleeding. I grip the shovel and wonder if we couldn't try once more to drive it out.

R.J. Sevin

NOT AT ALL
LIKE THE MOVIES

The two men sat in rusty fold-up lawn chairs, their useless rifles at their sides, a Dixie-Beer-filled cooler between them.

"Maybe it's all fake," Roy said, crushing an empty can and popping open another.

"It ain't fake. It's really happening." Carl looked around. Ten empty acres in the middle of nowhere, Louisiana. A dog barking. A distant lawn-mower buzzing. "Just not *here*."

"Mnnph," Roy said, belching into his mouth, his cheeks puffing.

"Yeah," said Carl, knocking back his beer.

Six weeks. Six *weeks* since the dead began to stand up and bite and Carl hadn't seen a single walking corpse.

"You see that video?" Roy asked after five minutes of silent drinking.

"Which one? The car accident?"

"Nah. The one with the kid in the morgue."

"Yeah."

There hadn't been much holding the kid's head onto his crumpled body, and the guy who brought his camera into the morgue seemed to have too much fun slapping it around the slab and playfully avoiding its champing teeth.

"I had to stop watching it," Roy said. "Too much. People are sick."

"Yeah," Carl said around his fifth beer. He lost count how many times he'd watched the video.

The news and online clips didn't count. It was something to see, yeah, dead people stumbling around with vacant eyes and slack jaws, yellowed and seeping flesh, missing limbs and spilling innards. But he wanted to *see* one.

Things weren't at all like they were in the movies. The dead were typically found in two places: hospitals and funeral parlors—nowhere else. The first week had been rough—or so said the news—but then folks more or less started doing what they were supposed to do.

In the movies, society would be crumbling and he'd be holed up in his house or in a mall or something. In reality, people did what they needed to do, and the world went on.

"You wanna drive around?" Roy asked.

"No point," Carl said. They'd driven around all last week, looking for accidents, almost getting in a few. No dice. Two weeks ago, Mr. Murphy down at the end of the road had died. By the time the news had reached them, Mrs. Murphy had already bashed in his skull with a meat tenderizer.

The sun sank, the mosquitoes came out. Roy stiffened, grabbed his gun.

Old Man Rideau crept down the road.

"Go to church," he yelled, waving. "World's ending." Nothing new there. He'd been saying that for years.

"Man," Roy said, sitting back. He opened another beer.

"Yeah," Carl said. He got another beer. He finished that one and got another.

"I wanted to shoot one tonight," Roy said, his words slurred.

"Me, too."

After his ninth can of Dixie, just after the woods ate the sun and the light above the work shed flickered to life, Carl picked up his rifle and blew Roy's heart through the back of the rusty fold-up lawn chair.

Then he waited.

Michael Josef

BRAVE

She must have died in her sleep, peacefully and quietly. She wasn't very ill, but the air is thick with it: the filth, the virus. The elderly don't stand much of a chance against it. When she went to sleep last night, she was my mother; now she is something else. Something that is trying to get into my room to infect me, kill me, eat me.

She scratches at the door. She doesn't say anything; her lungs don't work anymore. No more words of love and support from my mother's mouth. There is only disease, death, and another life.

She gave me life once, thirty-eight years ago. Now she can give me another or I can take this one away from her.

Looking through the boards I nailed across the window three years ago, I can see the dead walking; I can see the living knocking them down, spilling their brains and laughing. It has become status quo now. All I need to do is call out for help and my neighbors will come and bash in the head of the woman that raised me, fed me, read to me. I could call for help but I will hear them taking pleasure in it; then I will want to spill their brains, their blood.

The scratching is louder.

I have a gun. It's loaded, waiting on the bed. I could shoot through the door. I can imagine where her head is. I wouldn't have to see it explode, see her fall. Even though I know she isn't in that body anymore, it doesn't matter. It wears her face, has her hair. I could shoot her through the door; wait to hear her drop then run outside, never looking back. I could shoot myself.

I look out the window again. One of the shambling dead got hold of one of my neighbors, scratching him on the face and arm. Before the scratched man can react he is shot in the head by someone else in his group. It happens all the time, every day. No one looks too surprised or seems very upset by the death of their friend. It's like a game. Everyone will die. It's in the air, the rain, the blood. Whatever's spreading is doing its work fast. My mother is still scratching.

I thought I would be ready for this.

She told me a week ago to bring her the gun because she was feeling sick. She wanted to save me from having to do it. I looked into her eyes and told her I could do it. I told her that she wouldn't suffer when it came down to it, but I wanted her to get better. She made me promise. I remember her telling me when I was younger that where there is life, there is hope, and I almost forgot how she taught me to be brave. I just don't know what I will do without her.

I'll open the door.

Charles A. Gramlich
ONCE UPON A TIME WITH THE DEAD

Alkali dust under the white blaze of a Mexican sun.

Riders are coming. To a village standing idle on a ghostly quiet day.

Or so at first it seems.

Then, from the bell tower of the adobe church a lone guitar chord rings out. Quick fingers pluck a haunting tune. From one blank window comes a wink of silver. From another a *click-click-snap*. Men are waiting, good, honest men who are aware only that an old hatred is sweeping across their land.

The riders drift into the village square, long gray coats flapping in the dry wind that moves the dust. There are five of them. Known men. Wanted men who covet what doesn't belong to them. Men with strange, dangerous names like Doc, Clay, Jesse, Ringo, and Sundance. Their eyes are black, colder than the single-action Colts at their hips. The leader is Jesse. He dismounts, spurs chinking on the paving stones that mark the square.

That sound is a signal. The guitar clashes, strings shredding. From the windows of the town rifles speak smoke, and the rolling crack of gunfire hammers the brilliant sunshine. Bullets tug at gray dusters. A horse drops, and another, their riders leaping free, hands diving for pistols, coming up belching fire.

Jesse takes a shotgun slug to the chest, a .44 round through his shoulder. But his own guns are banging. Splinters and glass fly from the building above him. A man tumbles through a broken window, crashes through fleeing pigeons to the street.

The villagers are outmanned. This is not the evil they had expected. Their bullets tear holes in flesh and tattered gray, but it is only the defenders who fall, until they all lie crimson and still against a canvas of light and stark shadow.

But the gray riders?

They do not bleed.

They will not lie down.

Though dirt has been their friend before.

William T. Vandemark

THE BASEMENT

Julie screams. She's in the kitchen.

I'm in the basement stacking canned goods next to bottled water. I glance up at a barred window. Outside, misshaped figures shuffle past. I drop a case of Dinty Moore and run to the stairs.

"Get down here," I yell. "Right now or we're dead!"

Julie opens the door. She stands at the top of the stairs, pale with fear. She's claustrophobic. Yesterday, the idea of seeking refuge in a dank basement terrified her more than televised reports of zombies. This morning, the TV signal died.

Glass breaks—a picture window's timbre.

I take the stairs two at a time and grab Julie.

I pull, but she won't let go of the door jamb. Behind her, a wreck of a body appears, its face raw with shredded skin, mouth gaping. The zombie, teeth sharp and broken, lunges at Julie. I slam the door and throw the deadbolt.

A voice howls. Fingernails scratch at the door. The scrabble gives way to pounding.

I hit the door back. "Hah, you abomination. No way in!"

And no way out. I turn to Julie, who clutches one hand with the other. She's so pale, I'm afraid she will faint.

"It's okay," I say. "We'll hole up here. A few days, tops."

When I take her hands in mine, she cries out. They are warm and wet; the top joint of her index finger has been severed.

I swallow hard, resisting the urge to vomit. "Please tell me I did that with the door."

She rocks back and forth. "I don't know." Tears roll down her cheeks. They fall to the floor with drops of blood.

* * *

Hair unkempt, Julie is sitting on the floor, swaying, her jeans dark with stains. Ropes bind her wrists and ankles to bolts in the cinderblock wall.

With an X-acto knife, I slice my thumb and drip blood onto a sponge. I take the sponge to her cracked lips and paint them red. The whites of her eyes bulge like boiled eggs, then suddenly, I'm greeted with her amazing azure irises, the highlight of my day. For a moment, she looks straight at me, then shies away.

I reach out, but stop. She's trying to draw me in.

I'm under no illusion. If she had the chance, she'd sink her teeth into my Adam's apple.

She licks her lips, and her irises roll upward. She looks into the top of her skull. She moans, and her head lolls. Blindly, she snatches at air. Ropes tighten.

* * *

Outside, the world has fallen apart; my transistor radio hisses static.

Inside, sinew and bindings still hold.

Time crawls, the world whispers, floorboards creak. All the while, someone, some *thing*, still beats at the door, the thumping, an arrhythmia.

On good days, when Julie moans, I close my eyes and remember the times when such sounds came from other primal desires.

On bad days, I lean forward. Ever closer. Until her hot breath splashes across my throat.

Jeff Parish

JUST ENOUGH

Sneakers silent on the patio, Aaron pushed the glass door open, walked inside and closed it behind him. He crossed the office and leaned against another door, sliding to the floor with a sigh. He let one boy slip to the carpet and shifted the other, biting back a groan as his shoulder and elbow throbbed in protest. Jay snored softly. *Wish I could put him down*, he thought, then shook his head. The two-year-old would wake if he did. *Don't need him crying. Not with them so close.* Aaron gazed out the glass door, thumb working the hammer on a revolver in his waistband.

Zachary stirred at his side and peered up with bleary eyes. "Me hungy, Daddy."

"I know, buddy. We'll find something to eat later. Just be still for a bit, OK?" Aaron cocked his head. *What was that?*

The three-year-old pouted. "Want Mommy."

"Ssshhhh." There it was again, a distant but growing moan. He pulled the gun free and checked the cylinder. Two rounds. *Not enough.* He gave a humorless chuckle. When he'd snagged it and four boxes of bullets from the hotel manager's desk, it seemed a limitless supply. Now he had to get the three of them off the island with only two. *Not nearly enough.*

A herd of slack-jaws shuffled past the door, staring straight ahead. Aaron froze and clutched the boys. *Please, let them go by like last time.* He recognized some: fellow vacationers they'd sat next to at dinner a few days ago.

Another familiar figure shambled by. His breath caught.

"Mommy!" Zachary's shout shattered the silence. Several monsters halted. Aaron kept his gaze locked on the one that had been his wife. Long, stringy hair swung as her head swiveled from side to side. Aaron stood. Zachary wriggled and cried. "Me want Mommy!"

Jay jerked and wailed. Melissa's head snapped toward them. Drool dripped from her chin. She took a step forward, bumping into the glass door like a fly at a window. He heard her growl as she tried again and again.

Aaron shoved the struggling child behind him and groped for the doorknob. Zachary pushed himself free and streaked across the office.

"NO!" Aaron shouted. "Come back!"

He paid no mind, pulling the brass lever handle as Melissa bumped the glass again. The door swung inward. She grabbed the boy laughing and reaching up for her. Sobbing, Aaron wrenched the door behind him open and slammed it shut as Zachary's giggles turned to shrieks.

He wiped his eyes clear and turned to find himself in a storage closet.

The door rattled and thumped behind them. Groans arose on the other side. *Won't hold but a few seconds.*

He sank to the floor. There was no way out, not even an air conditioner vent he could shove Jay into. Aaron lifted the pistol and stroked the crying boy's head. He looked from the steel barrel to the rattling door and back.

A few seconds. Two rounds.

Just enough.

THE SONG OF *Lyca*

ART BY
SIMMONS
VERSE BY
WM. BLAKE

69

IN THE SOUTHERN CLIME,
WHERE THE SUMMERS PRIME,
NEVER FADES AWAY;
LOVELY LYCA LAY.

SEVEN SUMMERS OLD
LOVELY LYCA TOLD,
SHE HAD WANDERD LONG,
HEARING WILD BIRDS SONG.

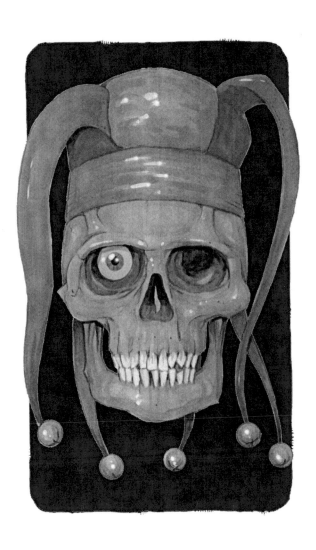

Matthew John Peters

HAROLD

Harold's zombie is throwing the office into a tizzy. And by "Harold's zombie," I don't mean the zombie-of-Harold, but literally Harold-the-zombie.

Harold died on Sunday of an aneurism—total blown fuse, lights out. He was, understandably, out on Monday, but, not understandably, he showed up at 8:10 Tuesday morning and filled out a missed punch slip. He didn't say anything besides a little grunt as if to say, "Morning," on his way from the time clock to his desk. And then he just sat there. All day. Except for the hour at lunch when he sat in the break room hogging the classifieds without reading them.

He came in on Wednesday, too. 8:15 this time, but didn't bother filling out a tardy slip. He went home early on Thursday for the funeral and we buried him that afternoon, but he was back at 8:05 Friday morning wearing jeans and a golf shirt for Casual-Friday.

He doesn't say anything or make any noise. Just sits there. He gets coffee, but doesn't drink it. If you ask him a direct question, like, "How you doing?" "Think it'll rain?" or "Where's the Goodrich order?" he lets out a full sentence worth of grunts, but you can't make out any of it. However, when you put a stack of orders in front of him, he'll process them. And quick, too. But if not, he just sits there watching his screensaver with that vacant stare. It's just like any other day working with Harold, except for him being dead.

And the office is in an absolute tizzy over it. HR doesn't know whether or not his benefits continue.

Accounting can't decide if they should be tracking his hours or not. *Should he still get a paycheck?* The people around him grumble that he smells but worry he'll get offended and eat their brains if they hang an air freshener on his cubicle wall. *Isn't that harassment?*

The custodians are the most upset. There's one heck of a mess: skin flakes and hair all over the desk, fingernails stuck in the keyboard, a bunch of unidentifiable stains on the floor. I heard last night they found maggots on his chair.

Surprisingly, management is being cool about the whole thing. They're inclined to keep him on as long as he gets his work done although they asked the company lawyers whether or not over-time pay requirements still apply.

Me? Hey, I'm just glad the vodou powder worked. I was going to miss Harold. That, and I didn't want to process all these orders by myself while HR dragged their butts for three months finding a replacement.

It was worth every penny.

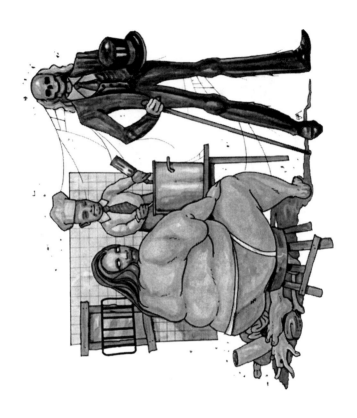

M.M. Johnson

BREAKING NEWS

"Ok," Terrence called from the van, "we are on in three . . . two . . ."

The transmitting light lit on Cal's camera telling John he was on. "Good evening, this is John Johnson reporting live from downtown. We are close to an intersection where police have set up roadblocks as they attempt to contain the unexplained violence gripping the area. Just moments ago, we witnessed the arrival of at least forty police officers dressed in full riot gear, who then marched into the affected area."

Cal waved his hand, pointing behind John.

"Hold on, it appears we have something happening," John said as he turned to look.

Cal zoomed in on the intersection; a city bus came into view with the early evening fog swirling around it. Police at the roadblock began shouting and signaling at the bus to stop.

The bus suddenly swerved to the left and ran onto the sidewalk, taking out a light pole and shattering several windows on its side. As the bus swerved back, someone tumbled from it. The man hit the ground hard and rolled across the pavement with his arms flailing about like a rag doll.

That guy's toast, Cal thought, but to his amazement, the man struggled to his feet and began lurching forward on obviously broken or severely injured legs.

The driver struggled with the steering wheel as the bus came up on two wheels and threatened to topple over, then righted itself. Still accelerating, it slammed into the barricade, shattering the front window. The barricade splintered like kindling as the hurtling bus tore through it, colliding with one of the police cars flipping it end over end. Two fleeing police officers disappeared beneath the twisted metal as it crashed to the ground.

"Oh no!" John cried. The bus sideswiped one of the police cars in the street and kept on. John could see the driver, a heavyset woman. Her teeth clenched in a wide open grimace, her eyes wide and bulging out of her blood-covered head.

"Terrence!" John screamed in panic.

Terrence, now realizing something was wrong, leaned out of the van just in time to see the front grill of the bus bearing down on him.

"Ahh!" Terrence cried as he tore his headset off and leaped from the van only seconds before the bus smashed into it.

Bursting out of the swirling mist moments later, a rider appeared like a ghost from a dark fairy tale.

"A pale horse," John whispered in awe, "and his name that sat upon him was Death." However, the rider was not the fabled angel of death, rather a mounted police officer.

The rider approached them at a breakneck gallop, and as he passed the news crew he screamed, "They're coming! They're killing everyone! Run for your lives!"

"And Hell followed with him," John finished as the first people began to appear from the mist beyond the roadblock.

Tim Waggoner

HARVEST TIME

"How about this one?"

You stop and look at the skeletal thing your sister has pointed out. Mottled flesh hanging loose on bones, mouth gaping, thick gray tongue protruding between cracked, leathery lips. The thing's jaws work mechanically, teeth gnawing on the fat worm-tongue. It moans as it chews, pus-colored eyes rolling back in their sockets in a kind of ecstasy.

After a moment's thought you say, "Too skinny."

Your sister looks at you as if you're crazy. "What does that matter? We don't want the body."

As if you need her to remind you of that. You've both been coming here to gather heads for Dire Harvest since you were children. And even if you'd never been here before, the headless bodies lying scattered around the orchard—on their backs, knees in the air, foot-roots still buried in the rich soil—would make it obvious. But she's always been one to argue for the sake of arguing.

"I mean its face is too narrow. Besides, it'll chew that tongue completely off before long, and how will that look?"

The dead thing moans once more, as if to underscore your point.

"It'll look gross," she says, "which is what we want."

You sigh. "A *proper* Dire Harvest head should express the insignificance of life compared to the profound beauty of Oblivion. This—" you gesture toward the tongue-chewer— "expresses only one thing: 'I'm especially stupid, even for a dead man.'"

You turn away and look around the orchard, searching for something better, but before you can spot anything, you sense movement. You turn back around and see your sister step close to the dead thing. She bats away its weak, clutching fingers with one hand and raises the hacksaw to its neck with the other.

"This one will do," she says as she starts sawing. "And don't start in with your unholier-than-thou attitude . . ."

"But the Dire Harvest—"

"Is about honoring the Great Dark Ones in order to stave off our own deaths for another year. And one corpse head will do that as well as another." She shakes her own head. "I wish I hadn't come home for Dire Harvest this year. I should be spending it with my friends back at college instead of with my pain-in-the-butt brother who always over thinks everything."

The dead thing looks at your sister as she saws at its neck. It moans louder, but whether in pain or pleasure it's hard to say.

You make a decision. "I'm sorry. I know we haven't always gotten along, but I truly am glad you came back." You step toward her and reach for the hacksaw. "Here, let me help you."

* * *

You smile as you leave the orchard; fresh, red blood drips from the ragged neck wound of the head you've collected.

"You were right," you say to your sister, though she can no longer hear you. "One head *is* as good as another."

88

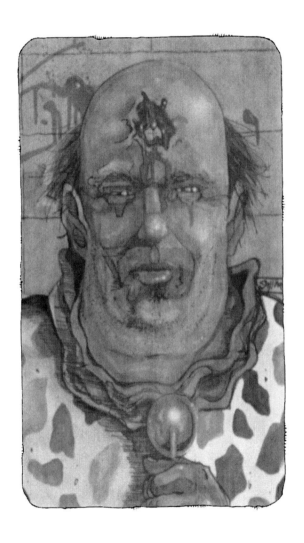

Daniel Pyle

FRESH MEAT

Morris watched from the shadowy alley as the group of zombies across the street lurched toward the apartment building's open doorway. His weapon was hot against his back, outlined by a band of sweat that had soaked through his T-shirt. There had been no electricity for weeks, no streetlights, but because the moon was almost full, Morris could clearly differentiate the monsters from one another. The lead figure had a gaping cavity where its internal organs had once been and a single loop of intestines hanging over the waistband of its shredded pants. Behind was a smaller horror that might once have been a woman. Its outer flesh was, for the most part, missing, leaving only the kind of androgynous musculature you found pictured in an illustrated encyclopedia. The third had just one arm and was leaning heavily to the side. It wore a Red Sox cap with a jagged bite taken out of the bill.

The zombies converged on the entryway and crowded through, their bare feet making little noise against the ground but their flesh smacking as they rebounded off one another and the doorframe. When they disappeared from sight, Morris abandoned his position and reached a hand over his shoulder. The sword came unsheathed with a soft, satisfying chime and reflected the moonlight when Morris swung it to his side.

He breathed through his mouth as he followed in the monsters' wake, and although he was still disgusted by their pungency, he managed not to gag and give away his element of surprise.

Moving with certainty, homing in on their prey with a hawk-like precision they shouldn't have possessed, the zombies burst into an apartment on the left, leaving splinters where a barricaded door had been.

Inside, moonlight shone through a curtainless window and Morris could see across the living room to a closed door on the other side. The sounds of movement from beyond it spurred the monsters on.

Morris struck out at Mr. One Arm first, punching the tip of the sword into the back of its Sox cap and pulling it free just as quickly. The zombie jerked sideways and fell. The thing's companions turned toward Morris, their faces slack and emotionless. Morris swung his weapon only once, angling the blade so that it took off the top of the taller zombie's head and then lodged in the skull of the short, skinned monstrosity. He stepped on the latter's face and used both hands to pull the sword free.

There was more movement behind the door. Morris went to it and turned the knob. In the bedroom beyond, he found two young women cowering together on the floor amid cans of food and plastic water jugs.

The post-apocalyptic world was hard for a man like Morris—slim pickings and all that—but if you followed the zombies long enough, they always led you to fresh meat. He grinned, hefted the sword, and stepped into the dark room.

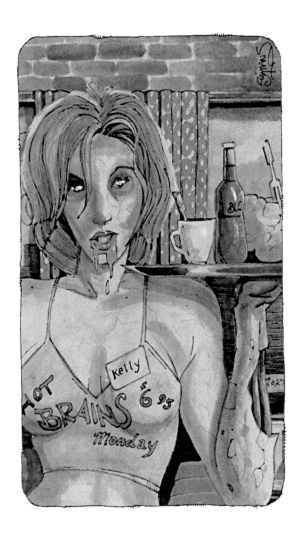

Nancy Kilpatrick

SICK

". . . and you being sick and all. I *told* you to let me drive! But no . . ."

Her voice pierced his skull. The sound ricocheted around his brain like something sharp and shiny, cutting, slicing, dividing; he had a vague memory of flashing silver. But more sounds were coming out of her, distracting him, sounds he couldn't make sense of. He struggled hard to concentrate.

Memories burst open, white-light flashes. Sick. He was sick. *Had* been sick. Was? Had been? He didn't know. A face, round, fatty, funny-looking. With effort he remembered Doctor Somebody at the clinic—

"You passed the mall! Stupid!"

Another violent sound! Inside his ears he felt a painful quiver. He turned to see where the sound came from. Someone sitting next to him in this space . . . this car . . . . He *knew* it was a car. *His* car. She turned towards him and her face, so full, so . . . succulent . . . . He opened his mouth and sound came out that to his ears was, "Aaaaha."

"What's the matter with you? Turn around!" she snapped. "Go back."

His head swiveled away from her, away from the sounds. Suddenly, things. Coming at him. Fast.

Then he noticed something round and two pale things on each side of it. Hands. He knew they were hands. A flash of light. *His* hands, skeletal. He had been sick. Off work. No more work. No more factory—

"Turn! You're gonna get us killed!" Stabbing!

The car spun and they headed somewhere else and now things were not coming at him but he was chasing after things. Cars? He *knew* that. Why did he keep forgetting? He was sick. A fever . . .

"Stop!"

The pulsing shriek chopped into his brain. Cleavers. Sharp wide blades struck here, there, hurting him. He remembered now. They had always hurt him. Always.

"Aaaaaaahhhhhhhhaaaaa." What he said and what it sounded like and what did he mean? He forgot.

". . . shopping, so you wait here for me!"

As he watched the form move away from him, something shifted.

Soon he trailed her, focused on her, all parts. What he saw before him spoke of need. Hunger. His. He accepted that now. Finally, something made sense!

She looked juicy. Tasty. Tantalizing. But he did not want to be tantalized. He wanted food. Everything in him demanded food. Eat or die.

She went through a door into a room and he followed and then followed again as she went into one of the small cubicles, but that door hadn't closed fully when he went in after her.

Shrieking. Knives. White light flash of kitchen knives slicing meat. Red. Raw. Bloody. All he wanted was the lips. Tasting them, sucking on them stopped the knives. And the hunger. And all the while he thought: *Sick*. But he didn't feel sick. Not any more.

Marcie Lynn Tentchoff

THAT BOY

They sent that boy to school again today. I'm not sure why they bother. There's a blank emptiness in his eyes that no amount of grammar or subtraction worksheets can fill. Perhaps it's just a matter of the law and his age. His kind are still so new in the public eye that some argue the same laws should cover them. Stupid, maybe, but no one asks teachers.

I gave him a little table all to himself near Jason and Quinn's. I hoped he'd maybe wake up a bit if I let him model himself on my most active pair of schoolyard delinquents. Instead, he spent the morning staring at his red crayon, just the tiniest trickle of drool running down his mottled gray chin. After a while even my two mischief makers grew quiet, and soon the whole class was working in a scarily studious silence, darting occasional spooked looks towards the boy at his lonely table.

The quiet should have been pleasant in my over-full classroom, but instead it just felt wrong. Lifeless.

When the recess bell rang things seemed more normal. He shambled out the door behind the usual mad rush of pushing, screaming kids, heading towards the blacktop area with its painted foursquare and hopscotch grids. Stuck on outside duty yet again, I sighed and shambled after him.

As I walked my regular patrol past monkey bars, swing sets, and sixth grade gossip areas, I tried to keep one eye on the boy where he stood not quite watching a foursquare game. So when Quinn's ball bounced off Stephanie's arm and rolled up to the boy's feet, I saw it, and might have done something if I'd not had both arms full of a weeping kindergartener, soothing her bruised knee and tattered ego.

"Throw it back." I could tell that Quinn was hiding fear behind the strength of his odor.

That boy just stood there, dark eyes unfocused, the ball resting against his grubby high-tops.

"I said throw the ball back. It's ours."

This time the boy seemed to hear, and perhaps to understand. He reached down, picking the ball up in his hands. His rotting flesh slid against the bright red rubber, smearing it with bits of slime and skin.

Stephanie made a loud gagging sound. Jason watched in fascinated disgust.

But Quinn, ruler of the second grade play area, was still trying to seem tough. "You're stupid. Sick. You don't belong with normal kids."

The boy stood still, holding the ball, looking nowhere, unanswering.

Quinn's voice rose. "Sicko. Dead boy. Go home!"

Slowly, as though the action was in no way related to Quinn's words, that boy raised the red ball to his mouth and bit.

The whistle of escaping air was covered by the ringing bell.

As he shambled past me into the classroom, I met that boy's eyes, just once. They've changed, I think. He *is* learning something here at school.

I'm just scared to wonder what it is.

Robert Appleton

CEMETERY

The *Hades* slowly orbited Earth. A hundred acres of soil and grass lay damp under the ribs of her roof. A faulty floodlight blinked overhead while giant fans whirred around the empty hall.

Wesley Orton frowned as he perused the ship's manifest. Five thousand and eighty-three names? *That's bizarre,* he thought. *Eleven too many.*

He didn't remember hitting his head or falling onto the wet soil, but he had woken, filthy, in the unfinished part of his cemetery.

Maybe there's someone else on board? His head pounded just above his left temple. *But surely I would've heard them.* He couldn't remember. Even the cold shower hadn't helped.

Wesley was the *Hades'* sole caretaker, the only soul on board. He had maintained the cemetery ship for fourteen years. He was forty-nine.

Sally Wainwright, Francesco Pirli . . . He marked all the names he didn't recognise. They were easy to spot. *After fourteen years, I ought to know . . .*

He'd made no mistake. Eleven names too many. He fell dizzy on his way to the cargo bay, where he found no evidence of unauthorized access. *Then what's happened?*

A shiny shovel he'd never seen before stood against Alice McGovern's headstone cross. Her grave was untouched, but Wesley couldn't bear to look further. He felt violated. He collapsed to his knees, disgusted. Plots all across the cemetery had been dug up, names he knew well, graves he'd cared for . . . desecrated.

Salty tears streamed to his lips. He felt ashamed.

He wandered by rows of empty graves. Pain jack-hammered his skull. Names on the headstones blurred as he passed while the rafters high above flickered from view and shadow veiled the far side of the cemetery.

Wesley stumbled toward the new section he had yet to finish. He gripped his temples and squeezed. The soil bore hundreds of footprints. Barely able to stand, he stared at a man's body lying facedown across the final, churned grave. The back of the shirt was not filthy. *He hasn't been dug up?* With trembling hands he turned the body over.

"Don't know you," he whispered. Checking the man's pockets, Wesley found a wallet. *Francesco Pirli.*

"One of the new ones?"

He glanced up at the headstone. His eyes widened. He slapped his face. Twice. *What the—?*

WESLEY ORTON.

With a cold shudder, he backed away from the body, into the shadow. The soil fumed. His back suddenly hit something. He turned. In the artificial gloaming, hundreds of decrepit figures huddled at the vast window. Some wore clothes, others bore nothing at all, not even skin. The awful smell overpowered him.

He ached deep inside. "*I* died? *I* killed Pirli . . . my replacement?" The memory flickered with the faulty floodlight.

The wreckage of an alien spacecraft hung from the *Hades'* roof. A viscous orange liquid dripped inside and out.

Among old friends, Wesley had never felt so lonely. But for the first time, he saw the faces of the names he knew.

They stared out longingly towards Earth.

J.G. Faherty
EXPERIMENTAL SUBJECT

Sick, sick, sicker. Illness in my mind, my body.

"*Leave me alone!*" I cry. "*Leave me alone. Stay away. Don't touch me.*"

But they don't understand. I hear, but I cannot speak. My mouth opens but no words come. Only sounds, gibberish.

The doctors talk about the impossible. Chemical activity. Functioning organs. Liver, heart, lungs, brain—all in advanced stages of putrification, but all working.

I understand them; why can't they understand me?

"There's no explanation for it," they say.

Don't try telling me why; I don't want to know. I just want it to end. It hurts, hurts all the time.

"*Let me die, please, let me die.*"

I make noise only to see it fall on deaf ears. The doctors point to me and say how my body continues to follow imprinted patterns from life. My family nods and cries at all the right places. "Do what you can."

No! Rescue me; someone, anyone. Take me from this place. This is not life. This isn't *right*. Wrong, all wrong.

Why are they doing this to me? Why won't they let me die?

* * *

More experiments. Surgeons. Knives. Needles. I don't feel them, yet my pain worsens. Fills me. The white coats talk of cures.

They lie. I know it.

They know it.

Nothing they do makes a difference. They remove things from inside me; inject chemicals into veins that no longer carry blood.

I scream, and no one cares.

* * *

A bed, rolling under yellow lights. How did I get here? Can't remember. The past is blurred; I see faces, but names escape me. Cold metal against my back. Doctors hover over me, more metal in their hands. They talk, they chatter. Ideas. Hypotheses.

Moths in the dark.

I remember something. The truth, but it's too late.

Why have they done this to me? Why was I chosen?

It doesn't matter anymore. Nothing matters.

The pain returns, stronger than ever. Blots out my thoughts.

The doctors turn away from me. Evil, plotting their next attack on my body. I can smell them. Blood, meat.

Food.

I finally recognize my pain—*hunger.*

I rise from the bed. I no longer care about their words. Only the pain matters. It must end.

They try to run but I am faster. Stronger. Soft flesh, fragile bones, no match for my hands and teeth. Their blood is hot and wet in my throat. I dig deep; find the parts that squish in my teeth.

As I eat, my mind remembers words again. Heart. Liver.

Brains.

Memories return. *Experimental Subject.*

They did this to me! The ones in the white coats.

I open the door and step into a bright hallway.

I will find them. *All* of them.
They put the pain inside me.
Now they will be the cure.

Adam-Troy Castro

AFTER THE ICE

The last thing Jason remembered before the ice shattered beneath his feet was the bitter December air, the zombies crossing the lake behind him, and the last living people in the world mere steps ahead on the shore, screaming at him to run faster. After that came only darkness.

A timeless time later he woke in bed and found himself safely behind walls in the compound clinic, surrounded by concerned faces.

Beautiful Margot clutched his right hand, tears streaming from her emerald-green eyes. "Thank God."

Jason coughed. "What happened?"

Dr. Friedgood said, "You were lucky. By the time we put down all those rotters, you'd been under for a full six minutes."

"It . . . shouldn't take . . . that long to drown."

"It didn't. You were gone. When we pulled you out and found that your heart had stopped, I didn't want to take the risk. I declared you dead and almost put the bullet through your head myself. Margot insisted that we try to revive you. There was only a small chance that the ice water had slowed your metabolism enough to minimize brain damage, so we were afraid that we'd have to take care of a mindless vegetable. But you came back to us, and our tests indicate that you're going to be fine."

Jason's best friend Cliff grinned. "Gotta hand it to you, pal. If you've got to come back from the dead, this is the way to do it."

Jason squeezed Margot's hand again, and fell asleep, which surprised none of the people around him.

Through the night he suffered dreams of the world before the apocalypse came, and dreams of the world it became after the dead rose with a hunger for human flesh—a nightmare world that he had only survived this long because his wife and friends had been there to support him.

When he woke the next morning, Margot had changed her clothes, putting on makeup and a tan sweater he'd always liked to see her wear.

She smiled. "Jason."

How happy she was. How happy they all must have been, when their friend and de facto leader escaped transformation into a zombie.

And so was he.

Who wants to be a zombie, mindless, shuffling, falling to pieces due to rot?

No, if he had to be hungry, if he had to be murderous, if he had to crave the taste of human flesh and the tang of human blood, if he had to have all of these wonderful things that had become part of his being in the short interval he'd been dead, it was better to be alive, to be loved, to be trusted, to be able to delay immediate gratification and to be able to plan.

He ran his fingers through Margot's long auburn hair. "As soon as I'm well, I'm going to love you like I've never loved you before."

She wept and kissed his hand.

Why not, he thought. It hadn't even been a lie.

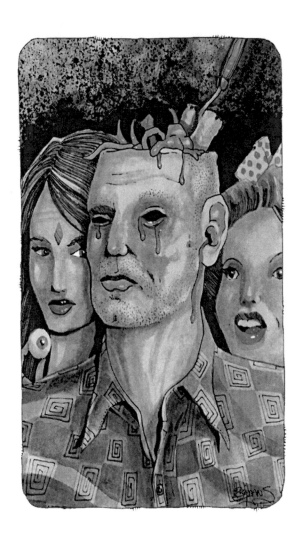

Kiernan Kelly

CLETUS

The trouble started earlier when my goldfish, Cletus, went belly up.

I wasn't particularly attached to Cletus. He wasn't the affectionate sort, being a fish, and I didn't really mourn his passing. I grabbed a small net and scooped his bloated little carcass out of the tank, intent on giving him a burial at sea courtesy of the commode.

I'd almost made it to the bathroom when the little bugger gave a shudder and started flopping in the net. Figuring I'd misjudged Cletus's state of health, I turned heel and carried him back toward the tank.

Without warning, Cletus flipped out of the net and onto my bare foot. It was then that I discovered a most curious fact.

Cletus had teeth—*sharp* ones.

He chewed a nice-sized hole in my instep before I dropkicked him into the afterlife for good, splattering him against the wall like a piece of yesterday's sushi. I slapped on a Band-Aid, swept Cletus's remains into the trash, and convinced myself that there had to be a reasonable explanation for what had happened. Perhaps the pet store had given me some sort of pygmy piranha instead of a goldfish.

I refused to acknowledge that Cletus's squishy remains continued to twitch inside my trashcan.

Later this afternoon I drove to the supermarket to pick up a few things. Wandering through the aisles, my attention was drawn to a commotion in the meat department. I had to elbow my way through the crowd to get a look at what was happening.

I immediately wished I hadn't.

Whole chickens were trying to kick free of their packaging, and I swear that a cow was trying to reassemble itself out of ribs, roasts, and sirloins. Then the lamb's head the butcher had displayed opened its mouth and took a chunk out of his right arm, along with at least three fingers.

Suddenly, I found I didn't have much of an appetite anymore. I rushed blindly out of the store along with the other customers and staff. People were running to their cars in a panic. Motors revved and brakes squealed as everyone tried to leave the lot at the same time. Metal screamed as cars collided with each other. Pedestrians flew through the air, landing in crumpled, bloody heaps.

For a minute or two, that is. Then they began to stir, much as Cletus had.

Cletus, I remembered, had had teeth.

So did the pedestrians—long, jagged ones that could chew more than a good-sized hole in my instep or any other part of my anatomy they might reach.

I dodged a gore-splattered woman who gnashed Ginsu-knife teeth at me. Jumping into my car, I navigated around smash-ups and shrieking people who were learning about the teeth the hard way. I drove home in record time.

I can hear Cletus twitching inside the trashcan, and there are things moving around inside my refrigerator.

My parents' ashes are in an urn in the living room.

I'm afraid to look.

C.M. Clifton
SURVIVAL OF THE FITTEST

Jake stiffened at the sound of the shuffling gaits above his head. He pictured the corpses staggering forward, driven by their need to feed, and he tightened his grip on his shotgun. All of the first floor window panes of the abandoned house he'd chosen this time were broken, so he could not rely on shattering glass to signal their arrival.

He straightened the night goggles fastened to his face and locked his gaze onto the bottom of the staircase leading to the basement. He had reinforced the door at the top of the stairs with his nail gun and several planks of plywood before his scent was detected that night. Yet, he always remained aware of the chance of his barrier failing.

A chorus of groans oozed through the air, and he retreated to a corner. Thankful the basement's small high windows remained boarded up, he uttered a silent prayer for the house's previous occupants, then listened for the *thuds* that usually signaled it was safe to leave his makeshift fort.

Seconds later, the distinctive sounds quieted the groans.

In the midst of the bloated silence, Jake's memory of chaos breaking out in the city slithered forward. Phantom screams echoed in his mind as he fought to refocus.

He stayed hidden, counting to the rapid beats of his palpitating heart. He rushed to the stairs on the count of ten, fired the shotgun and reloaded until the wood securing the door splintered, unconcerned with destroying it for a new dwelling had already been chosen.

Movement within the darkness of the kitchen leapt toward him.

He fell backwards as a Reanimate tackled him. Dagger-like teeth inches from his throat, he punched the thing's temple with the butt of his weapon. The blow only seemed to aggravate the creature as it hunched its spine, preparing to bear down on its prey.

Jake hurried to aim the shotgun between himself and the beast. He squeezed the trigger. The zombie's head exploded as its corpse flew back, lifeless at last.

Breathless from the battle, Jake forced himself to move on. He skulked to the living room.

He breathed through his mouth as he surveyed the massacre, the odor of decay hovering as if an infestation of rats lay dead within the walls. Heads, limbs, and torsos littered the room's weathered hardwood floor. Although none of the other Reanimates escaped the axes and machetes he'd rigged to ambush them, dead eyes rolled in the sockets of severed heads, arms inched forward guided by decomposed fingers, legs twitched, and torsos shivered.

Jake shot the heads, extinguishing the unnatural brain to body connection the Reanimates maintained beyond dismemberment and death. The other body parts grew still, and he set about collecting the least-decayed arms, legs, and torsos.

Although a last resort since the food supplies were depleted, the zombie meat kept Jake and the handful of survivors who shared his underground hideaway from starving.

Gina Ranalli

GRAY INVADERS

When she woke up dead, she was more angry than surprised. She'd thought she'd taken all the necessary precautions: locking herself in her third-floor apartment, ensuring that all doors and windows with street access were tightly secured. And she'd been satisfied that she'd done a good job of it, too. Short of a military onslaught, nothing was going to get inside her safe haven. Nothing, except for maybe the occasional infected flying insect, which had been said posed no danger at all.

Maddie knew that bit had been a lie when she discovered the red itchy welt in the crook of her left arm a few mornings ago. It was high summer, no electricity and she'd left the bedroom window open a few inches.

Now, dazed and drooling, she stood in her bathroom, glaring at her reflection in the mirror while all around her the sounds of a city in its death throes diminished with ever-increasing faintness. The screams were waning; the sirens mere memories.

Shaky fingertips touched the glass. Could that gray, dead thing in the mirror really be her? The waxen skin, blue irises several shades lighter than they had been in life. The dry, lackluster hair, falling out in places to float to the floor like dead autumn leaves, gravity alive and well on an otherwise wasted planet.

The only thing Maddie was aware of anymore was the hunger. The hunger and her inability to get to anything that would satisfy that gnawing, empty ache.

She'd tried prying the boards away from the doors, only to have first her fingernails snap off and then the fingertips themselves.

She was trapped in her self-made prison and the only emotion she seemed to have left was rage. Ripping through the cupboards for something—anything—alive to eat left her standing in the middle of the kitchen, boxes and cans strewn all around her feet, trembling with anger.

Absently, she scratched at the welt on her arm, felt the skin around the wound slide wetly away as yellow pus bubbled up and dribbled down her elbow, dropping to the floor with loud, flat smacks.

Maddie raised her arm closer to her face, head tilted with curiosity as the gray maggot squirmed its body through the widening black pit, its tiny body swaying first left, then right, searching for something. Fresh air, perhaps?

Alive.

Finally, something that was alive.

With thumb and forefinger, Maddie carefully plucked the maggot the rest of the way out of the wound and popped it into her mouth, chewing quickly, her gray tongue slipping out from between the cracked lips to catch a fleck of pus that had trickled free.

Food, at last.

Sinking into a sitting position amidst the wreckage of her kitchen, Maddie gleefully searched her body for open sores, digging her fingers deep within them, probing for that tiny blind morsel, even as *it* foraged for its own salty soft meal and a cool dark place to enjoy it in.

Jeff Strand

IMMUNITY

Believe me, I *howled* when that corpse—putrid meat dangling from its bones—sunk its teeth into the underside of my right arm. I won't say the pain was indescribable, since there are plenty of good descriptive words: excruciating, agonizing, unbearable, and so on. I'd seen friends, family, and strangers get bit, and even while they shrieked I'd never imagined it could hurt this much.

I pulled my arm away, leaving a strip of flesh in the zombie's jaws, and cried out for help. Not that it was necessary; my traveling companion Allen was right there. He shot the zombie in the head and it dropped. Then he looked at me sadly. "You know what has to be done."

No. No way. I'd been on the other side many times, but I wasn't going to let Allen murder me. I could fight off the infection. I knew I could. So before he had a chance to get over his moment of melancholy, I dove at him, tackled him to the ground, and pulled the gun out of his hand. Then I blew his brains out.

Heh. You didn't often see zombies shooting humans in the head.

Stop that. I wasn't a zombie. I'd never be a zombie. The others were weak. They succumbed to the infection because they believed what everybody said—you can't fight it. Well, I could fight it. I'd fight it and be stronger for the experience. I'd be an inspiration to The Bitten. A hero.

* * *

Not dead yet, so that was a promising sign. I'd been bit twelve hours ago, according to my watch, and I was the furthest thing from a shambling, mindless creature. The average time from bite to death? Two hours. But not me. Still alive and kicking, thank you very much. I was awesome.

* * *

Twenty-four hours. I didn't sleep during that time because that might've allowed the infection to overpower me, but I felt fine. My arm didn't even hurt.

I was immune.

Immune!

I was the key to humanity's survival! Whether it was something in my blood or my brain or whatever, I possessed the ability to withstand a bite from one of those things and not become one myself.

I needed to find people. There were scientists studying what was happening, and I could be the link to a cure. The zombies would eventually lose their spot at the top of the food chain, and life would return to normal. They'd build statues in my honor. Write songs. Name cathedrals.

I slowly walked through the forest, feeling pretty darn legendary.

* * *

The little girl screamed when she saw me. So did her mother.

I tried to tell her that I was okay, that I was immune, that I was humanity's savior, but my voice didn't work—

it was merely a soft groan. I wanted to weep as I fed upon the little girl's flesh, but there were no tears, just hunger.

Ed Dempster

CARSON'S END

The good people of Carson's End converged beneath the gallows where the body of Jack Carson, founder of the town, twisted in the breeze. He'd been declared dead by Doc Brown four weeks prior, but didn't show any intention of resting in peace. From day one he'd insisted on being cut down and set free, and when the Sheriff refused, Carson resolved to sing "She'll Be Coming 'Round the Mountain" until he did. He sang tunelessly, day and night, and only stopped for as long as it took to heckle passers by.

"Shut up, Carson," said Mayor Doohan. "Us decent folks are tryin' to decide what we're gonna do with you."

"Say, I don't s'pose one of you do-gooders got a swill of whisky for me? I'm parched after all that singin' and swingin'."

The judge thought for a moment and said, "Strictly speaking, Carson was sentenced to hang by the neck until dead, so if Doc Brown says he's dead, and boy he sure smells like it, then technically he's served his sentence."

"Yeah," said Carson, "about the smell—I asked for a fresh pair o' pants afore, on account of me filling this here pair when I dropped through the hatch, but . . ."

"Didn't I tell you to shut up?" said Mayor Doohan. "I can't hear myself think with you jabbering away in the background the whole time."

"Well 'scu-u-u-se me fer chippin' in, yer highness." Carson took a deep breath and began to sing, "She'll be . . . comin' round the . . ."

The crowd yelled, "Shut up!"

"Well cut me down then—I'm bored. It's bad enough being dead and all without having to hang around and listen to a bunch of do-gooders while I'm sober as a judge." He winked at the judge, who stiffened and put a hand to his flask pocket.

Carson's eyes widened, his body twitched and jerked, choking sounds issued from his throat. He fell limp.

The crowd gasped.

Mayor Doohan nodded to Doc Brown. "Check him out."

Doc Brown examined the body. "Like I said before, his neck's broke, heart's stopped, he ain't breathing—he's dead."

"That's right," said Carson, "I'm dead, so cut me down. Y'all heard the judge—I served my sentence and now it's time to let me go. I got a date with Rosey over at the saloon. Heck, I'm gettin' wood just thinkin' about her plump thighs wrapped around me, or maybe it's rigor mortis of the Johnson . . ."

The crowd gasped again. Ladies of the temperance league fainted en-masse.

"Oh don't come that crap," said Carson. "Y'all sinners just the same as me. I thought this was gonna be a fun place until all the hypocrites turned up and settled here, changed all the rules and gotten all high and mighty. In case you done forgot, I was the founder of this here place. Well, I wasn't so much founder as 'finder' of it. All the buildings were already here. What you'd call a ghost town, you know? Clue's in the name, in case you don't got it yet. We all dead."

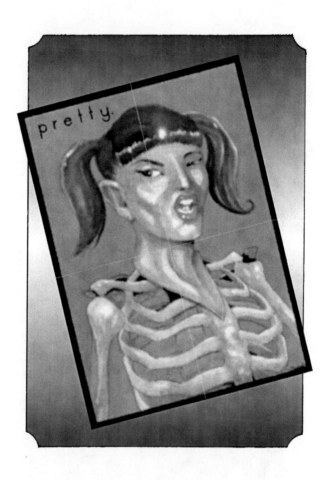

Catherine MacLeod

ZOMBIE SEASON

The secret's all in the salt. People just expect the town zombie hunter to carry it, along with a shotgun and squirt-bottle of gasoline. I don't believe it'll protect me, but if carrying it makes folks feel safer that's fine.

Of course, I've always carried salt; but not for reasons that would make anyone feel safe, and that's fine, too.

The first shriek shreds the air at 7 A.M., and I'm ready. I was a gravedigger, back before Judgment Day put me out of a job—no use digging holes if the deceased aren't going to stay in them—and these days people say I just have a natural way with the dead. Privately, I don't think much of their appetite for living flesh, but I don't judge.

Some people fear the dead, no matter what, and back then I didn't understand. Now I do. The dead know too many secrets, and some folks have reason to worry.

Like Adam Wade saying his crazy wife ran off to New York, only to have her shamble on home with her head stove in. Or the preacher's pure-as-new-snow daughter dying of pneumonia, then wandering into church yesterday with the remains of a dead baby caged in her ribs.

But everyone has secrets. I suppose how bad they are is just a matter of opinion.

Then again, concern for opinion has always kept me closemouthed about my own.

My seven o'clock job is a zombie on Main Street, who probably wouldn't even have noticed Miretta Jackson if she hadn't started screaming at it. Then again, it's Henry

Jackson, Miretta's late husband. She screamed at him non-stop when he was alive, and old habits die hard.

I shoot him down, spare the gasoline, and drop a match on the chance that—yup, you can always tell who's been embalmed; they go up like marshmallows.

I watch the fire from the coffeehouse as I eat pancakes and ketchup. The waitress, Gina, says, "Billy Martin, I swear you have no taste," just like always. Then, like always, she glances at my shotgun and moves off.

It's coming on fall now, and the dead slow down in cool weather. They're no good at all in winter. I'll have to start curing meat to put by while the hunting's still good. Gina has no idea, saying I have no taste. After all, isn't my salt mixed with parsley and thyme?

Life is easier these days. I don't have to dig the dead up anymore, or worry about getting caught; and no one wants to watch me roast zombies, especially when one might be their own dearly-departed. Still, I'm discreet. Only the dead know my secret, and I doubt they'll judge.

People say I just have a natural way with the dead, and I think that might be true.

That, and the secret really is all in the salt.

Kurt Newton

REAP

A soft squeal carried through the mist. Jeff shrugged on his shirt as he stepped out into the backyard. It was early yet. The morning sun hovered in the sky behind a layer of white gauze waiting to burn through.

The squeal came again only this time was followed by a muffled mewling. Jeff walked in the direction of the sound, toward the rose garden. Jennifer's rose garden.

Jennifer, his wife, loved her rose bushes. She raised them from ugly claws into beautiful bouquets. Every year, when the cold crept in, Jeff had watched her tie the dead canes together, mounding soil and leaves at their base to protect them. Every year, when spring melted the winter freeze, she pruned and clipped until the roses returned full as ever, yielding perfect blossoms and releasing their sweet perfumed scent across the yard.

Every year until the plague wind came and the newly dead bloomed worldwide.

Jeff tried not to think about the plague as he approached the garden. In the mist the circle of stones looked like a giant necklace. He remembered painting the stones white that first year, he and Jennifer setting them into place after she had planted her first bushes. There was something magical about putting things into the earth and watching them grow. In the years since, the rose garden had survived so much. Spring rains, summer windstorms. It had even survived the trampling it received last fall when the hunting parties waded through the yard, mistakenly killing Jennifer along the way.

The noises multiplied. It almost sounded like speech, but Jeff knew that couldn't be possible. The rose bushes appeared out of the mist. This year their stems had returned thick and fleshy; their leaves had adopted the shapes of tiny hands. Their unopened buds were no longer teardrop-shaped promises, but full blooms the color of blood. Their fragrance was that of dead meat. The blossoms swiveled their heads as Jeff drew near.

Jeff fell to his knees and wept.

Each delicate swirl of petals was shaped into an uncanny likeness of Jennifer's face. The sounds they made were hideous. They were the sounds of haunted dreams. It was the language of the dead, the language of the damned.

"I'm sorry, sweetheart. I thought it was what you would have wanted," he cried.

But just as love had interfered with Jeff's decision then, it clouded his thoughts now. He should have gone to the shed, retrieved the can of gasoline and burned these abominations as he should have burned her body last year. But instead he reached out to the nearest bloom for one last kiss.

Remarkably, the petals were as soft as her lips once were. He barely felt her tiny teeth as they rose up from inside and bit through his mouth.

In a matter of seconds, her fragrance became all-consuming, the words she spoke an invitation to paradise. He reached out and she grabbed hold of him then, and welcomed him back into her bed.

Nick Cato

TIGHT SPACE

Wearing a suit and tie is claustrophobic enough with having to stand in a crowded funeral home. But my aunt Delia was always good to me, so I put the nice-act on as I shook hands and kissed relatives I hadn't seen in over twenty years.

When I kneeled down before Aunt Delia's coffin, something wasn't right. I pretended to pray, but the color of her face was odd, even for a deceased woman. I eventually closed my eyes and started reciting the Lord's Prayer the best I could remember it—

—at first I thought my uncle Joe (Delia's husband) was tapping me on the shoulder, as if I was taking too much time. But when I opened my eyes, my aunt Delia's mouth was wide open and coming toward my face. I backed up, thinking I was having a temporary hallucination.

My ears quickly went deaf from people screaming. My uncle Joe ran by me and grabbed his wife by the shoulders.

"Delia! My prayers have been—"

The room panicked worse when Delia took a bite from my uncle's cheek, exposing the inside of his mouth. His shriek caused me to dig into my pocket and swallow two Xanax dry. I followed the crowd of hysterical mourners to the exit, only to find the funeral director slamming the deadbolt shut.

"What are you doing?" one of my cousins cried, ready to punch the man out.

"Get back! There's a bunch of crazy people in the parking lot! Get outta the way so I can lock the back door!"

The overweight director ran through us. I pried myself over to the window and saw countless slow-moving shapes gathering around the funeral home. Across the street, two of them were dragging what looked like separate parts of a child's body.

Judging from the distant screams, I knew the director was too late securing the rear entrance. Within a minute, the main hallway was full of filthy people who walked like mummies, blood covering most of their hands and faces.

While everyone scrambled for the basement's rest area, I jumped back into the wake room. My aunt was on her knees pulling her husband's insides out, sucking them down like spaghetti.

I had to think fast.

Fighting my worst fear, I snuck around Delia, climbed into her coffin, and quietly lowered the lid.

Good thing my watch lit up: after an hour of listening to my relatives scream in mind-numbing agony, I took another two Xanax.

My last two.

I held the lid down as best as I could when I heard them come into the room. Ten minutes passed when I heard the first muffled moans, then scratches atop the coffin.

I prayed they'd give up and leave, that they wouldn't figure out how to pull the wooden box open. Then I prayed the Xanax would mask my claustrophobia for as long as possible.

Steven Savile
THE DEAD CAN'T COOK

Herbert Loop stood in the quiet of what had been a thriving kitchen, the heart of his old restaurant. He stared at the heap of unwashed pans, imagining the hustle and bustle that used to be . . . before . . . before it all fell apart.

Rind and peel and mould curled and festered on the draining board, adding their own astringent reek to the air.

He lifted a trembling hand, dislodging the sauce pans as he tried to pull the flat pan free. Hunger ate away at his belly. The pangs were so fierce he could barely think. Parched lips parted, tasting the fetid air. His worm-tongue licked across those dry lips. He tried to swallow but the reflex was as dead as the rest of him. Herbert Loop almost dropped the pan as he shuffled wearily through the filth gathered on the kitchen floor. His fingers were too thick and clumsy to turn on the hotplate. He fumbled with the dial. Gas hissed into the air mixing with the other stinks and there was nothing he could do to stop it, so he listened to it hiss and breathed it in deeply. It was not as though a little gas could kill him again, could it?

It wasn't the mind that went first; it stayed painfully sharp. It was the body. The muscles atrophied, the nerves failed and taste buds degraded. The synapses misfired, dyskinetic twitches had him dropping anything his fat fingers couldn't feel or crushing them where he couldn't tell just how desperately he clutched them.

He was hungry.

All he wanted was to quiet the grumble of acids in his gut—but his digestive system was as dead as his heart. The food and drink sat in his belly, sloshing around. He couldn't pass it one way or another. Still none of it touched the gnawing hunger. He could eat and eat until he ruptured—there was nothing to stop him. Herbert Loop loved food. He was a master chef, Michelin stars and all. Food was life.

He took the knife, and the bell pepper, but could not control the cut. The knife spilled across the bench, rusted blade spinning, while the pepper rolled onto the floor. Herbert Loop grunted and ground a fistful of truffles between filthy fingers. He sniffed his hands. There was no lingering fragrance. They smelled of dead meat. Everything smelled of dead meat. Frustrated, he hurled the truffles at the pan. The gas still hissed.

He was so hungry.

He stared sadly at the rows of spices, at the garnishes and everything else that had been his life, the insatiable hunger tearing him apart. They were all too small, too fiddly, and the subtleties of his palette were gone. There was no point now. It all tasted like . . . like . . . death. He understood what drove the others now. They wanted to silence the thoughts! It was the compassion of the dead.

Herbert Loop abandoned his kitchen and shuffled out into the night, one word escaping his starving lips: "Brains . . ."

He was so very hungry.

149

Steve Vernon
WHISTLING
IN THE GRAVEYARD

It's funny, the things that'll eat at your heart.

My dad died three days after I turned thirty. I barely knew the man. He and Mom split up when I was three years old and left me with my grandparents. At best, Dad was an occasional stranger.

I got the telephone call in the dark of the night. His wife called. His heart took him.

"He'd been diagnosed last summer with bone cancer," she told me. "He was so afraid of what it would do to him. He went to ice fish this winter, same as every year. They found him lying on the ice. 'The heart,' the doctor said. I think he did it that way to look like an accident because of the insurance. He didn't want me to go hungry."

I dream of him sometimes lying there on the ice, belly down by the hole he'd augered, letting the cold gnaw into his heart, the tip-up dangling, waiting for a nibble. To this day I can't think of Dad without feeling that cold empty hole burning in my heart.

When I married Linda I swore it would be different. I never wanted to leave my son alone that way. She and I would stay together, no matter what.

Only there wasn't any son. We tried for years. Sometimes the seed doesn't take. Finally we stopped trying. She buried her grief. That empty womb ate at her, I knew it did, but through it all we stayed together.

Then the eaters rose up. The dead rose up out of their holes and began to eat us and when there were no more live ones they ate what ever was left.

Linda and I stayed together through it all. When they found us, when the first one bit her I let it bite me, too. And then, when the hunger took us we stayed together, wandering the streets of our town as a couple. Later, when live ones ran out, she and I walked into the woods. We lived off of what game we could walk down. Most of it was dead, too.

Then one morning I ate Linda.

The hunger grew too strong.

She let me do it. She didn't put up a fight.

I can still see her eyes, watching as I gnawed into her chest.

It took three whole days before she couldn't watch.

I don't know when she stopped feeling.

Now, I sit here alone in the snow and the darkness, gnawing on myself.

I started with my heart.

I dug a hole in my chest, rooting my fingers into the meat.

The meat tasted of Linda.

This taste and her memory is all I have left.

I sit in the snow, remembering Dad and remembering Linda, one mouthful at a time.

Soon, we'll be together again.

The wind whistles through me, a low hollow moan.

Jeffrey C. Pettengill
DEMOCRACY OF THE DEAD

Exiting the Holiday Inn on the Hill, Drake and Sarah Richardson were assaulted by the most nauseating stench.

"Ugh!" Sarah wrinkled her nose in disgust. "Are the garbage men on strike? It smells like the trash hasn't been picked up in a week."

"Not that I know of, Hon." Breathing through his mouth, Drake looked up New Jersey Avenue toward the Capitol building. He could see no garbage piled on the sidewalk. "Hopefully the convention center's shuttle will be here quickly so we can . . ." His voice trailed off as he looked in the other direction.

Shambling up the street was a horde of costumed people. Their costumes varied in specifics, but they were all faded, ragged and dirty clothes. The closer they drew, the more defined the people became.

"They've got the most amazing make-up I've seen outside the movies," said Drake awed. "It looks almost professional, so realistic. How'd they all afford such quality make-up jobs?"

"What the heck is it?" Sarah asked.

"A zombie walk I think," Drake responded.

"A what?"

"A zombie walk. People who walk together imitating zombies. I saw a news report on one."

"What a waste of time."

Drake shrugged and smiled. "Hey, it's not my idea of a fun time either. But then, I bet most of them don't get a charge out of scouring library book sales."

"How many are there?"

"I can't tell, but I'd guess several hundred."

Sarah clamped her hand to her mouth as the zombie walkers passed right in front of them. "That smell. I'm going to be sick."

"Can you make it back to the room?"

She shrugged, turned, and ran inside.

Drake started to follow, but paused as one of the zombie walkers' arms slipped from his sleeve and landed on the ground with a wet squish. The zombie walker continued walking.

Without thinking, Drake picked it up. His fingers sank deeply into bloated flesh.

That's not a rubber prop arm, he thought. A cold chill crawled slowly up his arm, as if the bodiless arm was a block of ice.

"He-he-here." Drake extended the lost arm to the walker, who turned its suppurating face and looked at him with eyes as dark and lifeless as a grave. An inarticulate moan issued from its open mouth along with maggot larvae.

Drake's bladder emptied.

The *real* zombie took its arm back just as a fist-sized pustule on its rotting cheek burst, covering Drake in its foul-smelling pus.

Drake screamed and fled.

* * *

The Richardsons sat horrified watching the news reports.

"The Capitol building is being overrun," the reporter pronounced.

All the stations carried C-SPAN's live cameras from inside the House of Representatives, showing the gory action. Hundreds of zombies tearing apart U.S.

Representatives, who were in the midst of an emergency session and taking their seats.

"I-I-I don't know how to describe what's going on," said the announcer. "It looks like the House seats are being claimed by zombies."

Taking David's hand, Sarah muttered, "Is anyone really going to know the difference?"

Simon Strantzas

TEN

Ten . . .

It has been so long that I can only remember this, my dear Rebecca. This house and our life within it. Even when I try, I cannot picture what came before. Was it even living at all?

Nine . . .

"The windows are strong," you said, hammer in hand, laughing as though you thought I could not see the joke. I saw it, my love. I just saw it too late.

Eight . . .

"I'll love you forever," you told me, and your eyelids fluttered with tears and then closed. My own tears did not stop, though. Not for hours.

Seven . . .

Do not fret. I held you all night as your body slowly cooled, and I kept holding you until the harsh light of day crept over your soft features and I felt your first tremble.

Six . . .

I knew you would tremble; you were so very cold.

Five . . .

When you opened your eyes and looked at me, did you feel what I felt? Do you remember me hugging you tight? Was it too tight to breathe? I ask, because you uttered a small moan, then pushed weakly against me, though I refused to let go.

Four . . .

My darling Rebecca. You and I have weathered so much together. I knew you'd never leave me.

Three . . .

I could not stay forever with you in my arms, as much as I wished it were otherwise. While you were still weak with slumber, I rose in the morning light. I smiled; kissed my fingertips; placed them on your forehead. You yawned, or were you playfully biting at them, my dear? I know you would never admit it.

Two . . .

In the closet, I found the toolbox, and smiled when I realized you had not returned the hammer I'd given you despite our wager. But I also wondered how I would fix the broken window now that it was gone, and the air outside was seeping in. I shook my head; I could worry about that later. For the moment, all I needed were the pliers.

One . . .

Only one tooth to go, my dear Rebecca, until I can kiss your lips once more.

ABOUT THEM WRITERS

Piers Anthony is an established author of fantasy and other genres. He lives with his wife of 52 years on a tree farm they own in the Florida backwoods. His website is www.hipiers.com

A poet turned fiction writer, **Robert Appleton** resides in Bolton, England. His first four novellas are under contract, including the sci-fi romance, *The Eleven-Hour Fall*, and its sequel, *The Elemental Crossing*, as well as *Esther May Morrow's Buy or Borrow*, a collection of paranormal short stories. He also has three more short stories, all science-fiction, awaiting publication in 2008. His work tends toward speculative fiction and exciting adventure. Readers will often find themselves in atmospheric settings—past or future—where human survival plays an instrumental role.

Joel Arnold lives in Minnesota with his wife and two kids. His work has appeared in venues ranging from *Weird Tales* and *Chizine*, to *American Road* and *Cat Fancy*. He also makes a mean coffeecake.

Drew Brown lives in England with his wife Serena. For more information about future releases, please visit www.myspace.com/drew_brown1981

Adam-Troy Castro's short fiction has been nominated for five Nebulas, two Hugos, and one Stoker. His novel *Emissaries from the Dead*, a science fiction murder mystery starring investigator Andrea Cort, is available from Harper Collins Eos. The sequel, *The Third Claw of God*, will be released from the same publisher in March 2009. Adam's other works include the horrific novella, *The Shallow End of the Pool*, released in 2008 by Creeping Hemlock Press. Adam lives in Miami with his wife, Judi, and a motley collection of insane cats.

Nick Cato's fiction has appeared in the anthologies *Deathgrip: Exit Laughing, Strange Stories of Sand and Sea, Southern Fried Weirdness (Vol. 1)* and in various web and print zines (including *Dark Recesses Press* and *Wicked Karnival*). With his wife Maria, Nick also runs Novello Publishers, a small press dedicated to humorous horror fiction, along with its bizarro-imprint, Squid Salad Press. Nick's debut novel will be here eventually . . .

Born where vampires are rumored to exist, **C. M. Clifton** lives among the bayous where mosquitoes can be saddled and Spanish moss droops from oak trees. Speculative and dark fiction are her favorite kinds of literature to read and write. She also enjoys editing the webzines, *Grim Graffiti* (www.grimgraffiti.com) and *Pen Pricks* (http://penpricksmicrofiction.grimgraffiti.com). She invites you to visit her personal site at www.geocities.com/black_ink_tales if interested in learning more about her and her fiction.

Christopher Allan Death currently resides in the concrete jungle of Northern Colorado. He has published fiction in *Worlds of Wonder, Night to Dawn, 7th Dimension Magazine*, and *Shallow Graves Magazine*, among others. You can find him at www.myspace.com/christopherdeath

Ed Dempster enjoys intellectual pursuits—he likes the way those clever people scream and cry when they see him chasing them with a meat cleaver. He lives in the depths of rural Somerset (England) with his longsuffering wife and kids. If you would like to look him up on the Internet, you can find him at www.cafedoom.com, where he runs a "behind the scenes" critique group for aspiring writers. Someday he plans to write the ultimate horror novel.

J.G. Faherty's 2008 publications include *Cemetery Dance*, *Wrong World*, *Shroud Magazine*, and several anthologies. You can visit his website at www.jgfaherty.com, and contact him at jg@jgfaherty.com. His non-fiction columns, interviews, and book reviews can be found in the HWA newsletter, *FearZone.com*, *Dark Scribe*, and *Horror World*.

Paul A. Freeman was born in London and works as an English teacher in Saudi Arabia. He is a regular contributor of short stories to *The Weekly News*, a UK newspaper. His crime novel, *Rumours of Ophir*, set in Zimbabwe, is on that country's "A" level English Literature syllabus and has been translated into German. He recently finished a trilogy of crime novels set in the Middle East, and the first installment, *Vice and Virtue*, is scheduled for publication in German translation this fall. He is married with three children.

Keith Gouveia is an author for today's reader. Some of his more memorable projects include the recently released *The Goblin Princess* from Lachesis Publishing, the Halloween chapbook *Devil's Playground*, co-written with A.P. Fuchs, as well as *On Hell's Wings*, and *Children of the*

Dragon, all published by Coscom Entertainment. He can be found on the web at www.keithgouveia.com

Charles Gramlich grew up on a farm in Arkansas but moved to the New Orleans area in 1986 to teach psychology at a local university. He's since sold four novels and numerous short stories, mostly in the genres of horror and fantasy. Charles has also published poetry and nonfiction. He lives with his wife in Abita Springs, Louisiana, and has a son named Joshua. His blog is at: http://charlesgramlich.blogspot.com

J.H. Hobson writes in the damp gray reaches of the Pacific North West. Her tales of the dead, the undead or the very nearly dead may be found in *Dead Letters*, *Bewildering Stories*, *Every Day Fiction*, *War Journal*, *History is Dead* (Permuted Press), *Loving The Undead* (From The Asylum Press), and *Black Box* (Brimstone Books). Ever since she saw her first dead dog when she was kid, the idea of one of them walking around undead, with all those huge teeth in its face, has really bugged her.

M.M. Johnson is a prototype tool mechanic living in Warren, M.I., with his wife and two teenage children. He is the author of, *The Black Empty's Letters from the Dead*, read by Dr. Pus on *Library of the Living Dead* at: www.dr-pus.podomatic.com. Stories written by M.M. Johnson can be found in the Free Fiction section on the Permuted Press website at: www.permutedpress.com/smf under the name: The Black Empty.

Kiernan Kelly is the published author of several novels in the frightening genre of romance—yes, even zombies fall in love, apparently. Kiernan's latest release is a historical romance titled, *In Bear Country II: The Barbary Coast*. Links to this and all of Kiernan's work can be found at www.kiernankelly.com

Award-winning author **Nancy Kilpatrick** (www.nancykilpatrick.com) has published 17 novels, close to 200 short stories and has edited 8 anthologies. She writes mainly horror, dark fantasy, mysteries and erotica. Upcoming stories will appear in these anthologies: *Blood Lite*; *Darkness on the Edge*; *The Living Dead*; *Zombies: The Walking Dead*.

Michael Laimo has written the novels *Fires Rising*, *Dead Souls*, *Atmosphere*, *Deep in the Darkness*, *The Demonologist* and *Sleepwalker*. His short stories have been collected in *Dark Ride, Demons, Freaks, and Other Abnormalities,* and *Dregs of Society*. He's recently completed another horror novel, and is currently working on a thriller. Visit him at myspace.com/michaellaimo

Catherine MacLeod lives in Nova Scotia. Her publications include short fiction in *On Spec*, *Solaris*, *TaleBones*, and several anthologies. Having seen herself in the mirror first thing in the morning, she has great sympathy for zombies.

James Newman lives in North Carolina. His published works include the novels *Midnight Rain*, *The Wicked*, and the short-story collection, *People are Strange*. Scheduled for release later this year is his latest novel, *Animosity*, as well as a limited-edition novella, *The Forum*. James invites readers to visit his website at www.james-newman.com, but says he hangs out more frequently on his MySpace page, www.myspace.com/newmanjames

Kurt Newton is the author of two short story collections, *The House Spider* and *Dark Demons*, one novel, *The Wishnik*, and the poetry collection, *Life Among the Dream Merchants*. His second novel, *Blood Alchemy*, is scheduled to appear in early 2009 from Delirium Books. He lives with his wife and two children in the northeast corner of Connecticut.

Jeff Parish is a 30-something native Texan. He and his wife have a girl and two boys. He started writing in middle school, where he concentrated mostly on (bad) fantasy tales and (even worse) poetry. His writing skills developed over time, much to his delight and the relief of everyone he forced to read his work, and he gravitated to prose over poetry. Jeff eventually decided to make a living as a writer, starting work at a small newspaper in Texas nearly a decade ago.

Matthew John Peters earned his MFA in fiction from the University of New Orleans in 2006. As stereotypical as it sounds, the idea for *Harold* came to him in the shower and he wrote the first draft while wearing only a towel.

Jeffrey C. Pettengill is from New England where he uses his day job as an accountant to subsidize his covert activities as a writer. He is enjoying life as he lives it, fostering his own passions and the passions of others. This is his first published short story.

Daniel Pyle lives in Springfield, Missouri, with his wife, Amy, and their newborn daughter, Dakota. Daniel has published more than a dozen short stories and has begun the agent hunt for his first novel, *Dismember*. You can visit him online at www.danielpyle.com

Gina Ranalli has contributed fiction, poetry and essays to countless anthologies, journals and zines. Her books include *Chemical Gardens, Suicide Girls in the Afterlife, Wall of Kiss* and *13 Thorns* (with Gus Fink.) She lives in Seattle and you can visit her on the web at www.myspace.com/ginaranalli

International bestselling novelist **Steven Savile** has written for *Doctor Who, Torchwood, Primeval, Stargate* and other television shows and movies, including *Return of the Jedi* and *Jurassic Park II: The Lost World*, as well as his own award-winning fiction. He is currently working on *London Macabre*, the first novel-length outing of the *Greyfriars Gentleman's Club, Snuff*, a crime noir forthcoming from Full Moon Books, and *Silver*, due in hardcover in the summer of 2009.

Julia Sevin (s'-VAN) is an expatriate Californian now braving the rooster-infested jungles of southeastern Louisiana. Too creative (or impatient) to commit to one trade, Julia has in recent years founded a small press, co-edited the Stoker-nominated anthology, *Corpse Blossoms*, dabbled in fine art, dived into graphic design, taught preschoolers, managed a newsstand, and made gourmet coffee. She enjoys the art and design best. Visit her at www.creepinghemlock.com or julia_sevin.livejournal.com

R.J. Sevin once loved the walking dead. He still does, truth be told—just not as much as he did back in the day, when there weren't fifty zombie books available and the thought of a new Romero *Dead* flick brought smiles instead of groans. He was born and raised in the shadow of New Orleans, surrounded by horror movies, monster masks, sex, drugs, and rock 'n' roll. He's written off and on since 1990, when he began writing his first (abandoned) novel—a zombie tale (surprise!) set in hurricane-ravaged New Orleans. He's currently nudging his first (completed) novel through its fourth draft. It may or may not have something to do with zombies.

Sean Simmans is a writer/tattooist/illustrator residing somewhere in Saskatchewan.

Nate Southard is the author of the novella, *Just Like Hell*, and the graphic novels, *Drive* and *A Trip to Rundberg*. His first novel will see print in 2009. He lives in Austin, Texas, with his girlfriend. You can learn more fascinating tidbits at www.natesouthard.com or www.myspace.com/natesouthard

Jeff Strand's novels include *The Sinister Mr. Corpse, Casket For Sale (Only Used Once), The Haunted Forest Tour,* and the Bram Stoker Award-nominated, *Pressure.* He thinks it would be just swell if you'd visit his *Gleefully Macabre* website at www.jeffstrand.com

Simon Strantzas has published over twenty short stories in places such as *Cemetery Dance* and Stephen Jones's *The Mammoth Book of Best New Horror* series. His first collection, *Beneath the Surface,* is due in September 2008 from Humdrumming Books, and he also writes a weekly blog at www.strantzas.com. He lives in Toronto, Canada.

Marcie Lynn Tentchoff is an Aurora Award-winning writer whose work has appeared in such publications as *On Spec, Weird Tales, Aeon,* and *Talebones.* Her poetry collection, *Sometimes While Dreaming,* is available through

Sam's Dot Publishing. Marcie lives in a small, seaside town on the west coast of Canada in a house surrounded by thick, shadowy underbrush and various wild creatures, most of them living.

Lee Thomas is the author of *Stained*, *Parish Damned*, *Damage*, and *The Dust of Wonderland*. In addition to numerous magazines, his short fiction has appeared in the anthologies *A Walk on the Darkside*, *Unspeakable Horror*, and *Inferno*, among others. He has won the Bram Stoker Award and been a Lambda Literary Award Finalist. Writing as Thomas Pendleton, he is the co-author (with Stefan Petrucha) of *Wicked Dead* (HarperTeen), a series of edgy horror novels for young adult readers. His novel, *Mason*, is also forthcoming from HarperTeen. Look for him on the web at www.leethomasauthor.com

William T. Vandemark can be found wandering the backroads of America in a van powered by vegetable oil. He chases storms, photographs wind vanes, and holds impromptu outdoor classes in solar observation. Wayward picnickers show their thanks by supplying him with chicken wings and potato salad.

Steve Vernon has been writing horror fiction for an awfully long time. His first full length novel, *Gypsy Blood*, will be released by Five Star in July 2008. His novellas, *Plague Monkey Spam* (Bad Moon Books) and *Leftovers* (Magus Press), are also 2008 releases. Lastly, pick up one of Steve's Nimbus Publishing ghost story collections— either *Haunted Harbours* or *Wicked Woods*—both available on Amazon or at Maritime bookstores.

Tim Waggoner's latest novel is the supernatural thriller *Cross County* from Wizards of the Coast Discoveries, and his latest short story collection is *Broken Shadows* from Delirium Books. He teaches creative writing at Sinclair Community College in Dayton, Ohio, and serves as a faculty mentor in Seton Hill University's MA in Writing Popular Fiction program. You can visit him on the web at www.timwaggoner.com

John Weagly is an award-winning writer with over 25 plays produced by theaters across the country and over 50 short stories and poems published in a variety of mediums. *The Undertow of Small Town Dreams*, a collection of his short stories, is available from Twilight Tales Publications. For more information about John, check out his website at www.johnweagly.com

Book One of the *Undead World Trilogy*

BLOOD
OF THE
DEAD

A Shoot 'Em Up Zombie Novel by A.P. Fuchs

"*Blood of the Dead* . . . is the stuff of nightmares . . . with some unnerving and frightening action scenes that will have you on the edge of your seat."

- Rick Hautala
author of *The Wildman*

Joe Bailey prowls the Haven's streets, taking them back from the undead, each kill one step closer to reclaiming a life once stolen from him.

As the dead push into the Haven, he and a couple others are forced into the one place where folks fear to tread: the heart of the city, a place overrun with flesh-eating zombies.

Welcome to the end of all things.

**Ask for it at your local bookstore.
Also available from your favorite on-line retailer.**

ISBN-10   1-897217-80-3 / ISBN-13   978-1-897217-80-1

www.undeadworldtrilogy.com

COSCOM ENTERTAINMENT

Where Imagination is Truth

www.coscomentertainment.com

Printed in the United States
144396LV00001B/14/P

9 781897 217818